THE THREE DRUGS

By

E. NESBIT

This edition published by Read Books Ltd.
Copyright © 2019 Read Books Ltd.
This book is copyright and may not be
reproduced or copied in any way without
the express permission of the publisher in writing

British Library Cataloguing-in-Publication Data
A catalogue record for this book is available
from the British Library

CONTENTS

___

E. Nesbit

Edith Nesbit was born in Kennington, Surrey in 1858. Her family moved around constantly during her youth, living variously in Brighton, Buckinghamshire, France, Spain and Germany, before settling for three years in Halstead in north-west Kent, a location which later inspired her well-known novel, *The Railway Children*. In 1880, Nesbit married Hubert Bland, and her writing talents – which had been in evidence during her teens – were quickly needed to bring in extra money.

Over the course of her life, Nesbit would go on to publish approximately 40 books for children, including novels, collections of stories and picture books. Among her best-known works are *The Story of the Treasure Seekers* (1898), *The Wouldbegoods* (1899) and *The Railway Children* (1906). Nesbit is regarded by many critics as the first truly 'modern' children's writer, in that she replaced the fantastical worlds utilised by authors such as Lewis Carroll with real-life settings marked by the occasional intrusion of magic. In this, Nesbit is seen as a precursor to writers such as J. K. Rowling and C. S. Lewis. Nesbit was also a lifelong socialist; in 1884 she was among the founding members of the influential Fabian Society. For much of her adult life she was an active lecturer and prolific writer on socialism.

Having suffered from lung cancer for some years, Nesbit died in 1924 at New Romney, Kent, aged 65.

THE THREE DRUGS

I

Roger Wroxham looked round his studio before he blew out the candle, and wondered whether, perhaps, he looked for the last time. It was large and empty, yet his trouble had filled it, and, pressing against him in the prison of those four walls, forced him out into the world, where lights and voices and the presence of other men should give him room to draw back, to set a space between it and him, to decide whether he would ever face it again—he and it alone together. The nature of his trouble is not germane to this story. There was a woman in it, of course, and money, and a friend, and regrets and embarrassments—and all of these reached out tendrils that wove and interwove till they made a puzzle-problem of which heart and brain were now weary. It was as though his life depended on his deciphering the straggling characters traced by some spider who, having fallen into the ink-well, had dragged clogged legs in a black zigzag across his map of the world.

He blew out the candle and went quietly downstairs. It was nine at night, a soft night of May in Paris. Where should he go? He thought of the Seine, and took—an omnibus. The chestnut trees of the Boulevards brushed against the sides of the one that he boarded blindly in the first light street. He did not know where the omnibus was going. It did not matter. When at last it stopped he got off, and so strange was the place to him that for an instant it almost seemed as though the trouble itself had been left behind. He did not feel it in the length of three or four streets that he traversed slowly. But in the open space, very light and lively, where he recognized the Taverne de Paris and knew himself in Montmartre, the trouble set its teeth in his

7

heart again, and he broke away from the lamps and the talk to struggle with it in the dark quiet streets beyond.

A man braced for such a fight has little thought to spare for the detail of his surroundings. The next thing that Wroxham knew of the outside world was the fact that he had known for some time that he was not alone in the street. There was someone on the other side of the road keeping pace with him—yes, certainly keeping pace, for, as he slackened his own, the feet on the other pavement also went more slowly. And now they were four feet, not two. Where had the other man sprung from? He had not been there a moment ago. And now, from an archway a little ahead of him, a third man came.

Wroxham stopped. Then three men converged upon him, and, like a sudden magic-lantern picture on a sheet prepared, there came to him all that he had heard and read of Montmartre—dark archways, knives, Apaches, and men who went away from homes where they were beloved and never again returned. He, too—well, if he never returned again, it would be quicker than the Seine, and, in the event of ultramundane possibilities, safer.

He stood still and laughed in the face of the man who first reached him.

'Well, my friend?' said he, and at that the other two drew close.

'Monsieur walks late,' said the first, a little confused, as it seemed, by that laugh.

'And will walk still later, if it pleases him,' said Roger. 'Good night, my friends.'

'Ah!' said the second, 'friends do not say adieu so quickly. Monsieur will tell us the hour.'

'I have not a watch,' said Roger, quite truthfully.

'I will assist you to search for it,' said the third man, and laid a hand on his arm.

Roger threw it off. That was instinctive. One may be resigned to a man's knife between one's ribs, but not to his hands pawing one's shoulders. The man with the hand staggered back.

'The knife searches more surely,' said the second.

8

'No, no,' said the third quickly, 'he is too heavy. I for one will not carry him afterwards.'

They closed round him, hustling him between them. Their pale, degenerate faces spun and swung round him in the struggle. For there was a struggle. He had not meant that there should be a struggle. Someone would hear—someone would come.

But if any heard, none came. The street retained its empty silence, the houses, masked in close shutters, kept their reserve. The four were wrestling, all pressed together in a writhing bunch, drawing breath hardly through set teeth, their feet slipping, and not slipping, on the rounded cobble-stones.

The contact with these creatures, the smell of them, the warm, greasy texture of their flesh as, in the conflict, his face or neck met neck or face of theirs—Roger felt a cold rage possess him. He wrung two clammy hands apart and threw something off—something that staggered back clattering, fell in the gutter, and lay there.

It was then that Roger felt the knife. Its point glanced off the cigarette-case in his breast pocket and bit sharply at his inner arm. And at the sting of it Roger knew that he did not desire to die. He feigned a reeling weakness, relaxed his grip, swayed sideways, and then suddenly caught the other two in a new grip, crushed their faces together, flung them off, and ran. It was but for an instant that his feet were the only ones that echoed in the street. Then he knew that the others too were running.

It was like one of those nightmares wherein one runs for ever, leaden-footed, through a city of the dead. Roger turned sharply to the right. The sound of the other footsteps told that the pursuers also had turned that corner. Here was another street—a steep ascent. He ran more swiftly—he was running now for his life—the life that he held so cheap three minutes before. And all the streets were empty—empty like dream-streets, with all their windows dark and unhelpful, their doors fast closed against his need.

Far away down the street and across steep roofs lay Paris, poured out like a pool of light in the mist of the valley. But Roger was running with his head down—he saw nothing but the round heads of the cobble-stones. Only now and again he glanced to right or left, if perchance some window might show light to justify a cry for help, some door advance the welcome of an open inch.

There was at last such a door. He did not see it till it was almost behind him. Then there was the drag of the sudden stop—the eternal instant of indecision. Was there time? There must be. He dashed his fingers through the inch-crack, grazing the backs of them, leapt within, drew the door after him, felt madly for a lock or bolt, found a key, and, hanging his whole weight on it, strove to get the door home. The key turned. His left hand, by which he braced himself against the door-jamb, found a hook and pulled on it. Door and door-post met—the latch clicked—with a spring as it seemed. He turned the key, leaning against the door, which shook to the deep sobbing breaths that shook him, and to the panting bodies that pressed a moment without. Then someone cursed breathlessly outside; there was the sound of feet that went away.

Roger was alone in the strange darkness of an arched carriage-way, through the far end of which showed the fainter darkness of a court-yard, with black shapes of little formal tubbed orange trees. There was no sound at all there but the sound of his own desperate breathing; and, as he stood, the slow, warm blood crept down his wrist, to make a little pool in the hollow of his hanging, half-clenched hand. Suddenly he felt sick.

This house, of which he knew nothing, held for him no terrors. To him at that moment there were but three murderers in all the world, and where they were not, there safety was. But the spacious silence that soothed at first, presently clawed at the set, vibrating nerves already overstrained. He found himself listening, listening, and there was nothing to hear but the silence, and once, before he thought to twist his handkerchief round it, the drip of blood from his hand.

By and by, he knew that he was not alone in this house, for from far away there came the faint sound of a footstep, and, quite near, the faint answering echo of it. And at a window, high up on the other side of the courtyard, a light showed. Light and sound and echo intensified, the light passing window after window, till at last it moved

10

across the courtyard, and the little trees threw back shifting shadows as it came towards him—a lamp in the hand of a man.

It was a short, bald man, with pointed beard and bright, friendly eyes. He held the lamp high as he came, and when he saw Roger, he drew his breath in an inspiration that spoke of surprise, sympathy, and pity.

'Hold! hold!' he said, in a singularly pleasant voice, 'there has been a misfortune? You are wounded, monsieur?'

'Apaches,' said Roger, and was surprised at the weakness of his own voice.

'Your hand?'

'My arm,' said Roger.

'Fortunately,' said the other, 'I am a surgeon. Allow me.'

He set the lamp on the step of a closed door, took off Roger's coat, and quickly tied his own handkerchief round the wounded arm.

'Now,' he said, 'courage! I am alone in the house. No one comes here but me. If you can walk up to my rooms, you will save us both much trouble. If you cannot, sit here and I will fetch you a cordial. But I advise you to try and walk. That *porte cochère* is, unfortunately, not very strong, and the lock is a common spring lock, and your friends may return with *their* friends; whereas the door across the courtyard is heavy and the bolts are new.'

Roger moved towards the heavy door whose bolts were new. The stairs seemed to go on for ever. The doctor lent his arm, but the carved banisters and their lively shadows whirled before Roger's eyes. Also, he seemed to be shod with lead, and to have in his legs bones that were red-hot. Then the stairs ceased, and there was light, and a cessation of the dragging of those leaden feet. He was on a couch, and his eyes might close. There was no need to move any more, nor to look, nor to listen.

When next he saw and heard, he was lying at ease, the close intimacy of a bandage clasping his arm, and in his mouth the vivid taste of some cordial.

The doctor was sitting in an armchair near a table, looking benevolent through gold-rimmed pince-nez.

'Better?' he said. 'No, lie still, you'll be a new man soon.'

'I am desolated,' said Roger, 'to have occasioned you all this trouble.'

'Not at all,' said the doctor. 'We live to heal, and it is a nasty cut, that in your arm. If you are wise, you will rest at present. I shall be honoured if you will be my guest for the night.'

Roger again murmured something about trouble.

'In a big house like this,' said the doctor, as it seemed a little sadly, 'there are many empty rooms, and some rooms which are not empty. There is a bed altogether at your service, monsieur, and I counsel you not to delay in seeking it. You can walk?'

Wroxham stood up. 'Why, yes,' he said, stretching himself. 'I feel, as you say, a new man.'

A narrow bed and rush-bottomed chair showed like doll's-house furniture in the large, high, gaunt room to which the doctor led him.

'You are too tired to undress yourself,' said the doctor, 'rest—only rest,' and covered him with a rug, roundly tucked him up, and left him.

'I leave the door open,' he said, 'in case you have any fever. Good night. Do not torment yourself. All goes well.'

Then he took away the lamp, and Wroxham lay on his back and saw the shadows of the window-frames cast on the wall by the moon now risen. His eyes, growing accustomed to the darkness, perceived the carving of the white-panelled walls and mantelpiece. There was a door in the room, another door from the one which the doctor had left open. Roger did not like open doors. The other door, however, was closed. He wondered where it led, and whether it were locked. Presently he got up to see. It was locked. He lay down again.

His arm gave him no pain, and the night's adventure did not seem to have overset his nerves. He felt, on the contrary, calm, confident, extraordinarily at ease, and master of himself. The trouble—how could that ever have seemed important? This calmness—it felt like the calmness that precedes sleep. Yet sleep was far from him. What was it that kept sleep away? The bed was comfortable—the pillows soft. What was it? It came to him presently that it was the scent which distracted him, worrying him with a memory that he could not define. A faint scent of—what was it? Perfumery? Yes—and camphor —and something else—something vaguely disquieting. He had not noticed it before he had risen and tried the handle of that other door. But now——. He covered his face with the sheet, but through the sheet he smelt it still. He rose and threw back one of the long french windows. It opened with a click and a jar, and he looked across the dark well of the courtyard. He leaned out, breathing the chill, pure air of the May night, but when he withdrew his head, the scent was there again. Camphor—perfume—and something else. What was it that it reminded him of? He had his knee on the bed-edge when the answer came to that question. It was the scent that had struck at him from a darkened room when, a child, clutching at a grown-up hand, he had been led to the bed where, amid flowers, something white lay under a sheet—his mother they had told him. It was the scent of death, disguised with drugs and perfumes.

He stood up and went, with carefully controlled swiftness, towards the open door. He wanted light and a human voice. The doctor was in the room upstairs; he——

The doctor was face to face with him on the landing, not a yard away, moving towards him quietly in shoeless feet.

'I can't sleep,' said Wroxham, a little wildly, 'it's too dark——'

'Come upstairs,' said the doctor, and Wroxham went.

There was comfort in the large, lighted room, with its shelves and shelves full of well-bound books, its tables heaped with papers and pamphlets—its air of natural everyday work. There was a warmth of red curtain at the windows. On the window ledge a plant in a pot, its leaves like red misshapen hearts. A green-shaded lamp stood on the table. A peaceful, pleasant interior.

'What's behind that door,' said Wroxham, abruptly—'that door downstairs?'

'Specimens,' the doctor answered, 'preserved specimens. My line is physiological research. You understand?'

13

So that was it.

'I feel quite well, you know,' said Wroxham, laboriously explaining—'fit as any man—only I can't sleep.'

'I see,' said the doctor.

'It's the scent from your specimens, I think,' Wroxham went on; 'there's something about that scent——'

'Yes,' said the doctor.

'It's very odd.' Wroxham was leaning his elbow on his knee and his chin on his hand. 'I feel so frightfully well—and yet——there's a strange feeling——'

'Yes,' said the doctor. 'Yes, tell me exactly what you feel.'

'I feel,' said Wroxham, slowly, 'like a man on the crest of a wave.'

The doctor stood up.

'You feel well, happy, full of life and energy—as though you could walk to the world's end, and yet——'

'And yet,' said Roger, 'as though my next step might be my last—as though I might step into my grave.'

He shuddered.

'Do you,' asked the doctor, anxiously—'do you feel thrills of pleasure—something like the first waves of chloroform—thrills running from your hair to your feet?'

'I felt all that,' said Roger, slowly, 'downstairs before I opened the window.'

The doctor looked at his watch, frowned and got up quickly. 'There is very little time,' he said.

Suddenly Roger felt an unexplained opposition stiffen his mind.

The doctor went to a long laboratory bench with bottle-filled shelves above it, and on it crucibles and retorts, test-tubes, beakers—all a chemist's apparatus—reached a bottle from a shelf, and measured out certain drops into a graduated glass, added water, and stirred it with a glass rod.

'Drink that,' he said.

'No,' said Roger, and as he spoke a thrill like the first thrill of the first chloroform wave swept through him, and it was a thrill, not of pleasure, but of pain. 'No,' he said, and 'Ah!' for the pain was sharp.

'If you don't drink,' said the doctor, carefully, 'you are a dead man.'

'You may be giving me poison,' Roger gasped, his hands at his heart.

'I may,' said the doctor. 'What do you suppose poison makes you feel like? What do you feel like now?'

'I feel,' said Roger, 'like death.'

Every nerve, every muscle thrilled to a pain not too intense to be underlined by a shuddering nausea.

'Then drink,' cried the doctor, in tones of such cordial entreaty, such evident anxiety, that Wroxham half held his hand out for the glass. 'Drink! Believe me, it is your only chance.'

Again the pain swept through him like an electric current. The beads of sweat sprang out on his forehead.

'That wound,' the doctor pleaded, standing over him with the glass held out. 'For God's sake, drink! Don't you understand, man? You *are* poisoned. Your wound——'

'The knife?' Wroxham murmured, and as he spoke, his eyes seemed to swell in his head, and his head itself to grow enormous. 'Do you know the poison—and its antidote?'

'I know all.' The doctor soothed him. 'Drink, then, my friend.'

As the pain caught him again in a clasp more close than any lover's he clutched at the glass and drank. The drug met the pain and mastered it. Roger, in the ecstasy of pain's cessation, saw the world fade and go out in a haze of vivid violet.

II

Faint films of lassitude, shot with contentment, wrapped him round. He lay passive, as a man lies in the convalescence that follows a long fight with Death. Fold on fold of white peace lay all about him.

'I'm better now,' he said, in a voice that was a whisper—tried to raise his hand from where it lay helpless in his sight, failed, and lay looking at it in confident repose—'much better.'

'Yes,' said the doctor, and his pleasant, soft voice had grown softer, pleasanter. 'You are now in the second stage. An interval is necessary

15

before you can pass to the third. I will enliven the interval by conversation. Is there anything you would like to know?'

'Nothing,' said Roger; 'I am quite contented.'

'This is very interesting,' said the doctor. 'Tell me exactly how you feel.'

Roger faintly and slowly told him.

'Ah!' the doctor said, 'I have not before heard this. You are the only one of them all who ever passed the first stage. The others ——'

'The others?' said Roger, but he did not care much about the others.

'The others,' said the doctor frowning, 'were unsound. Decadent students, degenerate, Apaches. You are highly trained—in fine physical condition. And your brain! God be good to the Apaches, who so delicately excited it to just the degree of activity needed for my purpose.'

'The others?' Wroxham insisted.

'The others? They are in the room whose door was locked. Look—you should be able to see them. The second drug should lay your consciousness before me, like a sheet of white paper on which I can write what I choose. If I choose that you should see my specimens—*Allons donc.* I have no secrets from you now. Look—look—strain your eyes. In theory, I know all that you can do and feel and see in this second stage. But practically—enlighten me—look—shut your eyes and look!'

Roger closed his eyes and looked. He saw the gaunt, uncarpeted staircase, the open doors of the big rooms, passed to the locked door, and it opened at his touch. The room inside was like the others, spacious and panelled. A lighted lamp with a blue shade hung from the ceiling, and below it an effect of spread whiteness. Roger looked. There *were* things to be seen.

With a shudder he opened his eyes on the doctor's delightful room, the doctor's intent face.

'What did you see?' the doctor asked. 'Tell me!'

'Did you kill them all?' Roger asked back.

16

'They died—of their own inherent weakness,' the doctor said. 'And you saw them?'

'I saw,' said Roger, 'the quiet people lying all along the floor in their death clothes—the people who have come in at that door of yours that is a trap—for robbery, or curiosity, or shelter, and never gone out any more.'

'Right,' said the doctor. 'Right. My theory is proved at every point. You can see what I choose you to see. Yes, decadents all. It was in embalming that I was a specialist before I began these other investigations.'

'What,' Roger whispered—'what is it all for?'

'To make the superman,' said the doctor. 'I will tell you.'

He told. It was a long story—the story of a man's life, a man's work, a man's dreams, hopes, ambitions.

'The secret of life,' the doctor ended. 'That is what all the alchemists sought. They sought it where Fate pleased. I sought it where I have found it—in death.'

Roger thought of the room behind the locked door.

'And the secret is?' he asked.

'I have told you,' said the doctor impatiently; 'it is in the third drug that life—splendid, superhuman life—is found. I have tried it on animals. Always they became perfect, all that an animal should be. And more, too—much more. They were too perfect, too near humanity. They looked at me with human eyes. I could not let them live. Such animals it is not necessary to embalm. I had a laboratory in those days—and assistants. They called me the Prince of Vivisectors.'

The man on the sofa shuddered.

'I am naturally,' the doctor went on, 'a tender-hearted man. You see it in my face; my voice proclaims it. Think what I have suffered in the sufferings of these poor beasts who never injured me. My God! Bear witness that I have not buried my talent. I have been faithful. I have laid down all—love, and joy, and pity, and the little beautiful things of life—all, all, on the altar of science, and seen them consume away. I deserve my heaven, if ever man did. And now by all the saints in heaven I am near it!'

'What is the third drug?' Roger asked, lying limp and flat on his couch.

'It is the Elixir of Life,' said the doctor. 'I am not its discoverer; the old alchemists knew it well, but they failed because they sought to apply the elixir to a normal—that is, a diseased and faulty—body. I knew better. One must have first a-body abnormally healthy, abnormally strong. Then, not the elixir, but the two drugs that prepare. The first excites prematurely the natural conflict between the principles of life and death, and then, just at the point where Death is about to win his victory, the second drug intensifies life so that it conquers—intensifies, and yet chastens. Then the whole life of the subject, risen to an ecstasy, falls prone in an almost voluntary submission to the coming super-life. Submission—submission! The garrison must surrender before the splendid conqueror can enter and make the citadel his own. Do you understand? Do you submit?'

'I submit,' said Roger, for, indeed, he did. 'But—soon—quite soon —I will not submit.'

He was too weak to be wise, or those words had remained unspoken.

The doctor sprang to his feet.

'It works too quickly!' he cried. 'Everything works too quickly with you. Your condition is too perfect. So now I bind you.'

From a drawer beneath the bench where the bottles gleamed, the doctor drew rolls of bandages—violet, like the haze that had drowned, at the urgence of the second drug, the consciousness of Roger. He moved, faintly resistant, on his couch. The doctor's hands, most gently, most irresistibly, controlled his movement.

'Lie still,' said the gentle, charming voice. 'Lie still; all is well.' The clever, soft hands were unrolling the bandages—passing them round arms and throat—under and over the soft narrow couch. 'I cannot risk your life, my poor boy. The least movement of yours might ruin everything. The third drug, like the first, must be offered directly to the blood which absorbs it. I bound the first drug as an unguent upon your knife-wound.'

The swift hands, the soft bandages, passed back and forth, over and under—flashes of violet passed to and fro in the air, like the shuttle of a weaver through his warp. As the bandage clasped his knees, Roger moved.

'For God's sake, no!' the doctor cried; 'the time is so near. If you cease to submit it is death.'

With an incredible, accelerated swiftness he swept the bandages round and round knees and ankles, drew a deep breath—stood upright.

'I must make an incision,' he said—'in the head this time. It will not hurt. See! I spray it with the Constantia Nepenthe; that also I discovered. My boy, in a moment you know all things—you are as God. For God's sake, be patient. Preserve your submission.'

And Roger, with life and will resurgent hammering at his heart, preserved it.

He did not feel the knife that made the cross-cut on his temple, but he felt the hot spurt of blood that followed the cut; he felt the cool flap of a plaster, spread with some sweet, clean-smelling unguent that met the blood and stanched it. There was a moment—or was it hours?—of nothingness. Then from that cut on his forehead there seemed to radiate threads of infinite length, and of a strength that one could trust to—threads that linked one to all knowledge past and present. He felt that he controlled all wisdom, as a driver controls his four-in-hand. Knowledge, he perceived, belonged to him, as the air belongs to the eagle. He swam in it, as a great fish in a limitless ocean.

He opened his eyes and met those of the doctor, who sighed as one to whom breath has grown difficult.

'Ah, all goes well. Oh, my boy, was it not worth it? What do you feel?'

'I. Know. Everything,' said Roger, with full stops between the words.

'Everything? The future?'

'No. I know all that man has ever known.'

'Look back—into the past. See someone. See Pharaoh. You see him—on his throne?'

19

'Not on his throne. He is whispering in a corner of his great gardens to a girl, who is the daughter of a water-carrier.'

'Bah! Any poet of my dozen decadents, who lie so still could have told me that. Tell me secrets—the *Masque de Fer.*'

The other told a tale, wild and incredible, but it satisfied the teller.

'That too—it might be imagination. Tell me the name of the woman I loved and——'

The echo of the name of the anaesthetic came to Roger; 'Constantia,' said he, in an even voice.

'Ah,' the doctor cried, 'now I see you know all things. It was not murder. I hoped to dower her with all the splendours of the superlife.'

'Her bones lie under the lilacs, where you used to kiss her in the spring,' said Roger, quite without knowing what it was that he was going to say.

'It is enough,' the doctor cried. He sprang up, ranged certain bottles and glasses on a table convenient to his chair. 'You know all things. It was not a dream, this, the dream of my life. It is true. It is a fact accomplished. Now I, too, will know all things. I will be as the gods.'

He sought among leather cases on a far table, and came back swiftly into the circle of light that lay below the green-shaded lamp.

Roger, floating contentedly on the new sea of knowledge that seemed to support him, turned eyes on the trouble that had driven him out of that large, empty studio so long ago, so far away. His new-found wisdom laughed at that problem, laughed and solved it. 'To end that trouble I must do so-and-so, say such-and-such,' Roger told himself again and again.

And now the doctor, standing by the table, laid on it his pale, plump hand outspread. He drew a knife from a case—a long, shiny knife—and scored his hand across and across its back, as a cook scores pork for cooking. The slow blood followed the cuts in beads and lines.

Into the cuts he dropped a green liquid from a little bottle, replaced its stopper, bound up his hand and sat down.

'The beginning of the first stage,' he said; 'almost at once I shall begin to be a new man. It will work quickly. My body, like yours, is sane and healthy.'

There was a long silence.

'Oh, but this is good,' the doctor broke it to say. 'I feel the hand of Life sweeping my nerves like harp-strings.'

Roger had been thinking, the old common sense that guides an ordinary man breaking through this consciousness of illimitable wisdom. 'You had better,' he said, 'unbind me; when the hand of Death sweeps your nerves, you may need help.'

'No,' the doctor said, 'and no, and no, and no many times. I am afraid of you. You know all things, and even in your body you are stronger than I. When I, too, am a god, and filled with the wine of knowledge, I will loose you, and together we will drink of the fourth drug—the mordant that shall fix the others and set us eternally on a level with the immortals.'

'Just as you like, of course,' said Roger, with a conscious effort after commonplace. Then suddenly, not commonplace any more—

'Loose me!' he cried; 'loose me, I tell you! I am wiser than you.'

'You are also stronger,' said the doctor, and then suddenly and irresistibly the pain caught him. Roger saw his face contorted with agony, his hands clench on the arm of his chair; and it seemed that, either this man was less able to bear pain than he, or that the pain was much more violent than had been his own. Between the grippings of the anguish the doctor dragged on his watch-chain; the watch leapt from his pocket, and rattled as his trembling hand laid it on the table.

'Not yet,' he said, when he had looked at its face, 'not yet, not yet, not yet.' It seemed to Roger, lying there bound, that the other man repeated those words for long days and weeks. And the plump, pale hand, writhing and distorted by anguish, again and again drew near to take the glass that stood ready on the table, and with convulsive self-restraint again and again drew back without it.

The short May night was waning—the shiver of dawn rustled the leaves of the plant whose leaves were like red misshaped hearts.

'Now!' The doctor screamed the word, grasped the glass, drained it and sank back in his chair. His hand struck the table beside him.

Looking at his limp body and head thrown back, one could almost see the cessation of pain, the coming of kind oblivion.

III

The dawn had grown to daylight, a poor, grey, rain-stained daylight, not strong enough to pierce the curtains and persiennes, and yet not so weak but that it could mock the lamp, now burnt low and smelling vilely.

Roger lay very still on his couch, a man wounded, anxious, and extravagantly tired. In those hours of long, slow dawning, face to face with the unconscious figure in the chair, he had felt, slowly and little by little, the recession of that sea of knowledge on which he had felt himself float in such content. The sea had withdrawn itself, leaving him high and dry on the shore of the normal. The only relic that he had clung to and that he still grasped was the answer to the problem of the trouble—the only wisdom that he had put into words. These words remained to him, and he knew that they held wisdom—very simple wisdom, too.

'To end the trouble, I must do so-and-so and say such-and-such.'

But of all that had seemed to set him on a pinnacle, had evened him with the immortals, nothing else was left. He was just Roger Wroxham—wounded, and bound, in a locked house, one of whose rooms was full of very quiet people, and in another room himself and a dead man. For now it was so long since the doctor had moved that it seemed he must be dead. He had got to know every line of that room, every fold of drapery, every flower on the wall-paper, the number of the books, the shapes and sizes of things. Now he could no longer look at these. He looked at the other man.

Slowly a dampness spread itself over Wroxham's forehead and tingled among the roots of his hair. He writhed in his bonds. They held fast. He could not move hand or foot. Only his head could turn a little, so that he could at will see the doctor or not see him. A shaft of desolate light pierced the persienne at its hinge and rested on the table, where an overturned glass lay.

22

Wroxham thrilled from head to foot. The body in the chair stirred—hardly stirred—shivered rather—and a very faint, far-away voice said:

'Now the third—give me the third.'

'What?' said Roger, stupidly; and he had to clear his throat twice before he could say even that.

'The moment is now,' said the doctor. 'I remember all. I made you a god. Give me the third drug.'

'Where is it?' Roger asked.

'It is at my elbow,' the doctor murmured. 'I submit—I submit. Give me the third drug, and let me be as you are.'

'As I am?' said Roger. 'You forget. I am bound.'

'Break your bonds,' the doctor urged, in a quick, small voice. 'I trust you now. You are stronger than all men, as you are wiser. Stretch your muscles, and the bandages will fall asunder like snow-wreaths.'

'It is too late,' Wroxham said, and laughed; 'all that is over. I am not wise any more, and I have only the strength of a man. I am tired and wounded. I cannot break your bonds—I cannot help you!'

'But if you cannot help me—it is death,' said the doctor.

'It is death,' said Roger. 'Do you feel it coming on you?'

'I feel life returning,' said the doctor; 'it is now the moment—the one possible moment. And I cannot reach it. Oh, give it me—give it me!'

Then Roger cried out suddenly, in a loud voice: 'Now, by God in heaven, you damned decadent, I am *glad* that I cannot give it. Yes if it costs me my life, it's worth it, you madman, so that your life ends too. Now be silent, and die like a man, if you have it in you.'

Only one word seemed to reach the man in the chair.

'A decadent!' he repeated. 'I? But no, I am like you—I see what I will. I close my eyes, and I see—no—not that—ah!—not that!' He writhed faintly in his chair, and to Roger it seemed that for that writhing figure there would be no return of power and life and will.

'Not that,' he moaned. 'Not that,' and writhed in a gasping anguish that bore no more words.

Roger lay and watched him, and presently he writhed from the chair to the floor, tearing feebly at it with his fingers, moaned, shuddered, and lay very still.

Of all that befell Roger in that house, the worst was now. For now he knew that he was alone with the dead, and between him and death stretched certain hours and days. For the *porte cochère* was locked; the doors of the house itself were locked—heavy doors and locks new.

'I am alone in the house,' the doctor had said. 'No one comes here but me.'

No one would come. He would die there—he, Roger Wroxham— 'poor old Roger Wroxham, who was no one's enemy but his own.' Tears pricked his eyes. He shook his head impatiently and they fell from his lashes.

'You fool,' he said, 'can't *you* die like a man either?'

Then he set his teeth and made himself lie still. It seemed to him that now Despair laid her hand on his heart. But, to speak truth, it was Hope whose hand lay there. This was so much more than a man should be called on to bear—it could not be true. It was an evil dream. He would wake presently. Or if it were, indeed, real—then someone would come, someone must come. God could not let nobody come to save him.

And late at night, when heart and brain had been stretched to the point where both break and let in the sea of madness, someone came.

The interminable day had worn itself out. Roger had screamed, yelled, shouted till his throat was dried up, his lips baked and cracked. No one heard. How should they? The twilight had thickened and thickened, till at last it made a shroud for the dead man on the floor by the chair. And there were other dead men in that house; and as Roger ceased to see the one he saw the others—the quiet, awful faces the lean hands, the straight, stiff limbs laid out one beyond another in the room of death. They at least were not bound. If they should rise in their white wrappings and, crossing that empty sleeping chamber very softly, come slowly up the stairs—

A stair creaked.

24

His ears, strained with hours of listening, thought themselves befooled. But his cowering heart knew better.

Again a stair creaked. There was a hand on the door.

'Then it is all over,' said Roger in the darkness, 'and I *am* mad.'

The door opened very slowly, very cautiously. There was no light. Only the sound of soft feet and draperies that rustled.

Then suddenly a match spurted—light struck at his eyes; a flicker of lit candle-wick steadying to flame. And the things that had come were not those quiet people creeping up to match their death with his death in life, but human creatures, alive, breathing, with eyes that moved and glittered, lips that breathed and spoke.

'He must be here,' one said. 'Lisette watched all day; he never came out. He must be here—there is nowhere else.'

Then they set up the candle-end on the table, and he saw their faces. They were the Apaches who had set on him in that lonely street, and who had sought him here—to set on him again.

He sucked his dry tongue, licked his dry lips, and cried aloud:

'Here I am! Oh, kill me! For the love of God, brothers, kill me *now!*'

And even before he spoke, they had seen him, and seen what lay on the floor.

'He died this morning. I am bound. Kill me, brothers; I cannot die slowly here alone. Oh, kill me, for Christ's sake!'

But already the three were pressing on each other at a doorway suddenly grown too narrow. They could kill a living man, but they could not face death, quiet, enthroned.

'For the love of Christ,' Roger screamed, 'have pity! Kill me outright! Come back—come back!'

And then, since even Apaches are human, one of them did come back. It was the one he had flung into the gutter. The feet of the others sounded on the stairs as he caught up the candle and bent over Roger, knife in hand.

'Make sure,' said Roger, through set teeth.

'*Nom d'un nom,*' said the Apache, with worse words, and cut the bandages here, and here, and here again, and there, and lower, to the very feet.

Then this good Samaritan helped Roger to rise, and when he could not stand, the Samaritan half pulled, half carried him down those many steps, till they came upon the others putting on their boots at the stair-foot.

Then between them the three men who could walk carried the other out and slammed the outer door, and presently set him against a gate-post in another street, and went their wicked ways.

And after a time, a girl with furtive eyes brought brandy and hoarse, muttered kindnesses, and slid away in the shadows.

Against that gate-post the police came upon him. They took him to the address they found on him. When they came to question him he said, 'Apaches', and his late variations on that theme were deemed sufficient, though not one of them touched truth or spoke of the third drug.

There has never been anything in the papers about that house. I think it is still closed, and inside it still lie in the locked room the very quiet people; and above, there is the room with the narrow couch and the scattered, cut, violet bandages, and the thing on the floor by the chair, under the lamp that burned itself out in that May dawning.